Thomas's Sheep
and the
Great Geography Test

Thomas's Sheep
and the
Great Geography Test

By Steven L. Layne
Illustrated by Perry Board

PELICAN PUBLISHING COMPANY
Gretna

*To my parents, Richard and Suzie,
for always believing.*
                        —Steven

*For Theresa. Let's visit some
of these places together.*
                        —Perry

*The word "Pelican" and the depiction of a pelican are trademarks
of Pelican Publishing Company, Inc., and are registered
in the U.S. Patent and Trademark Office.*

Library of Congress Cataloging-in-Publication Data

Layne, Steven L.
    Thomas's sheep and the great geography test / by Steven L. Layne ;
illustrated by Perry Board.
        p. cm.
    Summary: Worried about an upcoming geography test, Thomas finds
himself unable to fall asleep until he tries counting sheep.
    ISBN 1-56554-274-6 (hardcover : alk. paper)
    [1. Geography—Fiction. 2. Test anxiety—Fiction.] I. Board,
Perry, ill. II. Title.
PZ7.L44675Th 1998   97-15816
                                                                 CIP
                                                                  AC

Printed in Korea

Published by Pelican Publishing Company, Inc.
1101 Monroe Street, Gretna, Louisiana 70053

Thomas's Sheep
and the
Great Geography Test

Thomas could not sleep.

Tomorrow morning all of the boys and girls in Mrs. King's class would take her Great Geography Test, which covered twenty-six countries of the world. Mrs. King's students had been preparing for the test for weeks, but Thomas had been studying harder than anyone.

As he lay in his bed staring at the ceiling, Thomas tried to think of something, anything, other than the Great Geography Test!

He spied his little brother's bathtub toys lying near the closet,

but the more he looked at them, the more they looked like the shapes of the different countries he had been studying!

He tried having conversations with some of his stuffed animals, but they only wanted to talk about the different countries they came from.

Thomas was worried. He needed to think of a way to get his mind off of the Great Geography Test. How could he do well on the test tomorrow if he couldn't fall asleep tonight? Then Thomas remembered what his mother used to tell him when he was very small and complained to her that he could not fall asleep.

"When you cannot fall asleep, find your rest by counting sheep," his mother would say in a gentle voice. Then she would hold his hand, and they would begin counting sheep together.

Thomas had never tried counting sheep on his own. Would counting sheep be able to take his mind off of the Great Geography Test and put him to sleep? Certainly it would. "After all, what do sheep have in common with the countries on my test?" Thomas thought. He repeated his mother's words and decided to follow her advice.

Next, Thomas closed his eyes tightly and prepared for the count. He imagined an emerald green pasture enclosed by a rickety, old fence. The fence had turned a soft gray color like the one on his grandfather's farm.

At last it was time! Thomas conjured up his first sheep. "Naaah! Too plain," Thomas thought, and he erased the sheep from his mind.

After several more attempts, he finally came up with a style of sheep that he knew would hold his interest.

"Awesome!" Thomas exclaimed as he admired his creation.

He sent the first sheep over the fence without incident, and the second, and the third. But the fourth sheep ran into a bit of a problem because Thomas's pasture was filled to capacity. Sheep one through three, having nowhere else to go, had taken up all of the room! This left the fourth sheep in a very delicate situation with his front legs where he wanted to go and his hind legs still on the way there.

"Why doesn't anybody ever tell you what to do with these sheep once they jump over the fence?!" Thomas questioned from somewhere in a dreamlike state. As he tossed and turned in his bed, he realized that something had to be done with the sheep. That's when Thomas decided to send them off on adventures around the world!

They started off by doing a little acting in **Australia,** and they all landed leading roles!

Next, they were baking in **Belgium** . . .

. . . and canoeing in **Canada.**

They loved diving in **Denmark,** but they had to remind each other about proper form.

They followed the rules of etiquette while eating in **England,**

and fishing in **Finland** went fine once they got their hooks baited.

While they were golfing in **Guatemala,** one of the sheep scored a hole in one!

Soon they were hiking
in **Hungary,** ice skating
in **Iceland,** juggling in
Japan, and kayaking in
Kenya.

DANUBE RIVER
TRAIL 18 KM

When they needed a break, they tried lounging in **Liechtenstein.** But before long they were off again, and this time they went mountain climbing in **Mexico!**

Sadly, one of the sheep experienced difficulties with his map when they were navigating the Niger River in **Nigeria!**

They tried operating in **Oman,** but they weren't very successful.

Next, they went picnicking in **Peru** and quilting in **Qatar.**
Quilting isn't as easy as it looks.

They became excited about the reading they were doing in **Romania,** and the librarian had to remind them that libraries are quiet places.

The sheep loved skiing in **Switzerland,**

and they really showed some skill while they were typing in **Tunisia.**

They didn't have an easy time
unicycling in the **United States,**
but it sure was fun!

When the sheep began vocalizing in **Venezuela,** people came

They went water skiing in **Wales** just to get a break from all their fans!

The sheep tried to help with some x-raying in **Xinjiang,** but the people at the hospital didn't seem to think it was such a good idea.

The doctors sent them off to **Yemen,** where they began yodeling and caused a minor mishap.

They decided to finish their trip by zigzagging through **Zimbabwe.**

By the time they returned to their pasture, Thomas was fast asleep. And the next day . . .